I0670157

# The Adventures Of
# Ruby & Diamond
## "Journey to Rainbow Frost"

**Written & Illustrated**

**By: Tenille Jones**

One beautiful morning, the sun glistened so brightly upon Agape Island. It shined so bright that its beams laid out the most royal carpet that was ever made, hand crafted by the greatest craftsmen. It shined through the royal door of a very noble king named Jerome. He waited as his wife Queen Gloria was about to give birth to two of the greatest gifts.

As the hours passed, the sun stayed in the same position. A loud trumpet played, along with deep rooted African drums. The people of Agape Island gathered around the castle. As the doors opened, the sun beamed even brighter. There were two gorgeous ebony skinned twin girls with tight spongy hair that graced the crowd with their presence.

As the king lifted each one of the girls to the sky, the sunray kissed their beautiful brown skin even more. The two little princesses looked as if they were drawn by the greatest artist there ever was. They were as lovely as can be. Therefore, the king and queen named the girls after precious jewels.

"We would like to present to you, Princess Ruby and Princess Diamond!"

1

As the twins grew older, they were like two peas in a pod, inseparable. Even though the girls weren't able to speak actual words, it was very clear that they understood each other. Ruby would say something like, "ya da do da" which means to roll. Diamond's favorite saying would be ba ta ta ta ta which means milk time.

The unique words that were only understood by babies tickled the queen at times.  She would laugh so hard that her laughter would tickle the twins also.  They all laughed until they fell asleep.

Spring had arrived and seven years had passed.  The twins loved to dance their way around the island.  There was a beautiful waterfall called, Cyan Falls that sat on the outskirts of Agape Island. At the bottom of the waterfall, was a hidden treasure chest that the king had forbidden.  The girls would sit along the fall just to look at the beautiful sparkly chest.

Each day they became more and more curious.  Until one day they just couldn't take it anymore.   They swam toward a rock that sat under the fall.  Their eyes glistened as they walked up to the sparkly treasure chest.

As the girls moved their little fingers toward the latch of the chest, they quickly drew their hands away from it.  It was as if they heard their father's voice telling them not to touch the chest, but they were curious.  The beauty of the chest captured them.  Ruby tried to unlatch the hook but it didn't open.  Then Diamond tried but was unsuccessful also.

Ruby and Diamond grabbed the latch at the same time.  The glistening chest opened.  In the chest were two golden keys.  One had an engraved R and the other had an engraved D.  The chest also had two colorful sparkly batons.  The twin's faces lit up with smiles from ear to ear.

Ruby and Diamond grabbed the sparkly batons.  They danced and twirled them around the beautiful Cyan Falls.  While waving the batons, glitter sprinkled around the treasure chest.

Suddenly, the wind began to howl as the trees swayed back and forth.  The chest gleamed with beams of colorful lights.  As the girls backed away from the chest, there was a loud sound coming from the midst of it.  It was the sound of an elephant.

African drums begin to play, "boom, boom, boom!"

The girls backed up further away clinching the inner walls of the fall. The ground started to tremble! Beams of iridescent lights paraded its way out of the chest.

The last drum beat was played, "boom!"

The chest closed suddenly! There stood a large unidentified being under the misty falls.

The girls looked closely but couldn't make out what it was. It stood up on its hind legs and roared! As the midst cleared, there stood a big tall grand elephant. Her skin was beautiful, as black as night with elegant jewels draping her back.

As the elephant slowly walked toward the girls, it frightened them! They clinched onto one another closing their eyes hoping that this was all a dream. Ruby and Diamond opened their eyes realizing that it was reality. The elephant bowed to them.

"Hello Princess Ruby and Princess Diamond," said the elephant.

"A talking elephant?" asked the girls looking at one another in shock.

The girls fainted.

Ruby and Diamond awakened to a lumpy and bumpy ride on the back of the elephant.  The girls screamed and attempted to jump, but they were up too high.  The elephant came to a complete stop and lowered herself.  The twins quickly leaped off of the elephants back stumbling to the ground.

"Please don't hurt us!" the girls shouted.

"I'm not here to hurt you.  I'm here to protect you," replied the elephant.

"Well do you have a name?" asked Diamond.

"Ha, ha, ha everyone has a name.  My name is Sooney," said the elephant as she reached out her trunk.

Diamond whispered into her sister's ear, "Ruby, I think she's trying to eat us."

Ruby burst into laughter.  "No silly nilly she's only greeting us.  Nice to meet you Sooney," said Ruby as she walked up to the elephant and shook her trunk.

The elephant greeted her back.

After building up enough courage,

Diamond finally walked up to

Sooney to greet her.

Ruby, Diamond, and Sooney continued their journey. The twins looked around amazed at all of the iridescent lights.  There were rainbows arching from the sky.  Thin rivers coiled through the beautiful land.  All kinds of animals graced the land with their presence.  There were fuchsia flower trees greeting as they walked by.  The girl's eyes were large not missing a thing in sight.

"Wow, where are we Sooney?" asked the twin princesses.

"You are in the land of Rainbow Frost," replied Sooney.

Sooney lowered herself.  Ruby and Diamond jumped off of Sooney's back.  They danced and twirled their way around Rainbow Frost.

A beautiful voice sifted into the girls ears.  Her voice was as soft as a beautiful humming bird awakening in the morning dew.  The twins stopped and listened to the beautiful voice.

A little girl just as cute as can be walked toward the twins singing so pleasantly.  Birds congregated behind her as well as two weasels named, Nippy and Jippy.

As the little girl sang her last note, she reached out her hand to greet the twins.

"Hi Princess Ruby and Princess Diamond.  My name is Koloah."

"Hi Koloah," replied the girls.

The birds bowed to the princesses.

"How do you know our name?" asked Ruby.

"Who doesn't know your name? You're the Princesses of Agape Island," replied Koloah.

"You've been chosen to conquer The Madam Kruzabella," said Nippy and Jippy.

The twins looked puzzled.

"Wait a minute, first of all who is Madam Kruzabella and sorry you have the wrong Princesses because we can't fight.  See, let me show you, ha yah!" shouted Ruby kicking one leg up tripping to the ground.

"Ruby that was a really clumsy kick," said Diamond flushed with embarrassment for her sister.

Ruby jumped up dusting herself off.

"The point is we're not fighters, and maybe there are two other princesses that will be more than happy to conquer Madam Kruzabella," said Ruby.

"You know, it's really nice meeting you," said the twins.

"Ruby and I have to be on our way now," said Diamond pulling her sister by the hand.

The further Ruby and Diamond walked away, all they could hear was sniffling. Nippy and Jippy pulled out a flute playing the saddest song ever. Koloah's little voice began to sing so sadly. She had birds singing behind her.

"Diamond, don't look back," said Ruby with tears rolling down her face.

"Ok Ruby," replied Diamond with tears the size of grapefruits flooding her big beautiful eyes.

As they passed the big fuchsia flower trees, the tree's folded over belching out tears the size of ocean waves. Ruby and Diamond just couldn't take it anymore.

"Ok we give in!" they shouted.

"Yay!" shouted the people of Rainbow frost.

The next day Ruby and Diamond had awakened to a smell of sweet flappy cakes that were made by the elders. They had fresh fruits laid on top of them. After finishing the last touches, the elders laid out a large platter for the children.

They gathered around anxiously as the sweet smell of the flappy cakes sifted through their nostrils. A prayer was said before they proceeded to eat.

Every bite of the sweet savory flappy cakes melted in Ruby and Diamond's mouth. They were so good that some of the kids jumped up doing the happy dance. Sooney even joined them in the dance. After the flappy cakes were gone they all were nice and full.

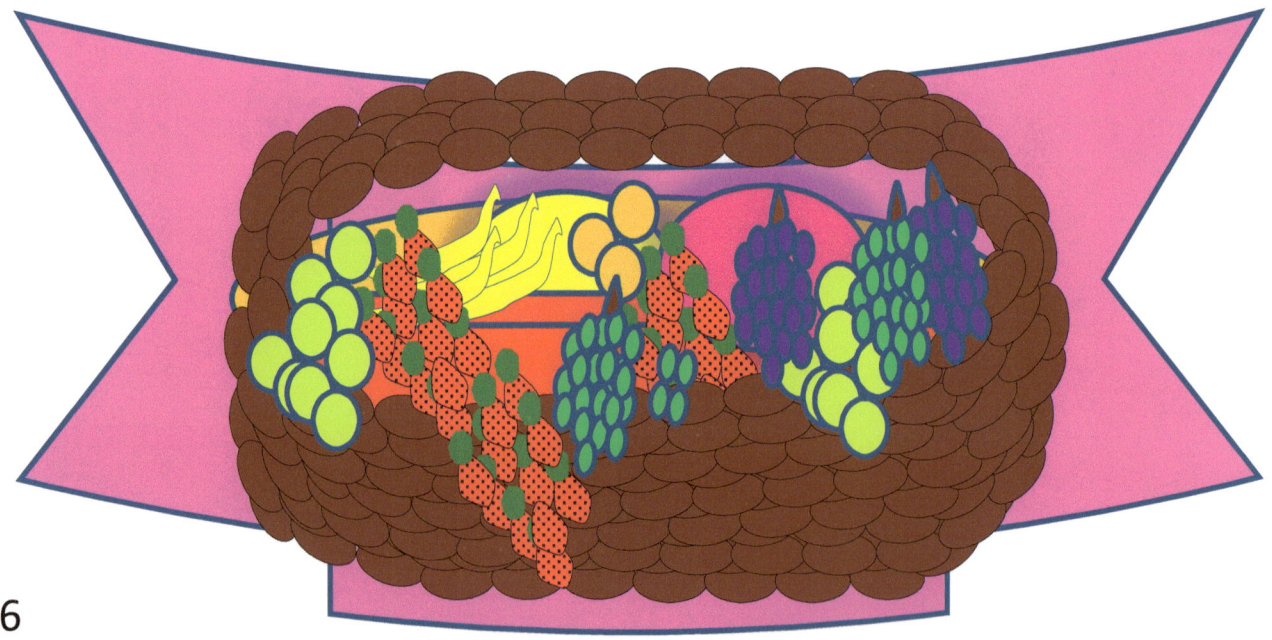

After breakfast, the kids swam in the thin coiled rivers.  Some climbed the vines and slid down the rainbow arches.  Others floated down the river on large elephant leaves.

Besides Agape Island, Rainbow Frost was more than anyone could imagine.  It was fantastic!

Ruby and Diamond continued their journey. They marched and sang down Frost Berry Lane.

"Sooney, where are we headed?" asked the twins.

"We are headed to Mount Frost to unlock the Great Rainbow," replied Sooney.

"What is the Great Rainbow?" asked the twins.

"The great rainbow is a protective gate that surrounded the outskirts of Rainbow Frost.  It stops anyone with bad intentions from entering," replied Sooney.

"Well isn't it still surrounding Rainbow Frost?" asked the twins.

"No my darlings, it is long gone.  You see years ago Kibble, who was the guard at the gate, was tricked by The Madam Kruzabella's beauty into letting her into the gates.  She then stormed into Rainbow Frost using her magic to take over some of the land, but she couldn't find the keys to take over all of it.  Therefore, she only took a portion."

"Where are the keys she's looking for?" asked the twins.

"You have them my dears," replied Sooney.

"Wait a minute, we're not going to be able to defeat a lady with magical powers," said the twins.

"Princess Ruby and Princess Diamond you've been chosen. Magic is only an illusion. You both have something that is far beyond magic and that is called faith that comes strictly from "The Great I Am." His power is far beyond measures. All it takes is for you to believe," replied Sooney.

Since it was night time Sooney guided the children over to campout for the night.

Bzzzzz, bzzzzz, bzzzz!

"Elica Bee, Jelica Bee!" Nippy and Jippy shouted.

Everyone jumped up franticly scattering in all directions.

"Hurry girls, jump on my back," said Sooney lowering herself.

Ruby, Diamond, and Koloah jumped onto Sooney's back.

"Whoa!" shouted the girls as Sooney flew off to safety.

"Who's Elica and Jelica Bee?" asked the twins.

"They're Madam Kruzabella's twin orphans daughters. The madam sent them to hit us with the stingy bees. Sooney watch out there's a stingy bee!" Koloah shouted.

"Girls hold on tight," said Sooney twisting and turning to avoid the stingy bees.

When Ruby and Diamond turned around, they saw twin girls galloping wildly on horses. They were winding their wands like a whip slinging out the stingy bees.

"What are we going to do Sooney?" asked the twins.

"Pull out your sparkly batons!" shouted Sooney.

Sooney lowered herself from the air galloping onto Frost Berry Lane.

The twins pulled out their sparkly batons pointing them at Elica and Jelica.

"It's not working!" screamed the twins.

"Remember girls, you have to have faith and to have faith you must first get rid of the fear," replied Sooney.

Koloah closed her eyes and began to sing.  Her voice started off a little shaky, but the more she sung the fear began to sift away.  The melody of Koloah's voice gave the girls strength.  This time when they pointed their sparkly batons, beautiful butterflies slowly drifted out of them.

For a split second the girl's belief began to fade.  They wondered how could a beautiful soft butterfly that floats pleasantly into the air could run away bees equipped with stingers.  There were only two options.  The twins could believe or not believe.  They decided to believe.

Butterflies drifted softly out of the sparkly batons.  When the bee's spotted them, they ran away with fear.  Elica Bee and Jelica Bee swerved the wild horses around and ran away.

 "Hip hurray!" shouted the children of Rainbow Frost.

The girls had defeated Elica and Jelica Bee for now but it wasn't over.

They continued their journey down Frost Berry Lane heading toward Mount Frost that held the Great Rainbow. The Twin Princesses were so amazed at how the little soft floating butterflies ran off the stingy bees.

Having faith was so amazing that the twins were now ready for anything that came their way.

Ruby and Diamond spotted a sign that changed from Frost Berry Lane to Madam Kruzabella Lane. They knew that they were getting closer and fear hit their bellies as misty rain drizzled on their faces. As they approached the line, Sooney was the first to cross over.

"Do not cross this line if you're going to be afraid, because faith can't operate with fear," said Sooney.

Ruby took a deep breath and crossed the line.

Diamond and many others followed one by one except for Nippy and Jippy. Their teeth chattered as if it was on a cold winter's night.

"Come on Nippy and Jippy we need you," said the twins.

"Oh no, we don't mess with the Madam," replied Nippy and Jippy.

"Nippy and Jippy, do you know who you are?" asked Sooney.

"Ah yeah, were weasels," answered Nippy and Jippy.

"Of course you are but you are also more than a conqueror, above and not beneath, the head and not the tail says "The Great I Am," replied Sooney.

"We are, even though we're small?" asked Nippy and Jippy.

"Yes, all you have to do is have faith at least the size of a mustard seed to move a humongous mountain. Isn't the size of a mustard seed really small and you're small right?" asked Sooney giving Nippy and Jippy something to think about.

"Yes," they answered.

"Nippy and Jippy step across this line," said Sooney.

Nippy and Jippy teeth were still chattering, but they braved it out and stepped across the line.

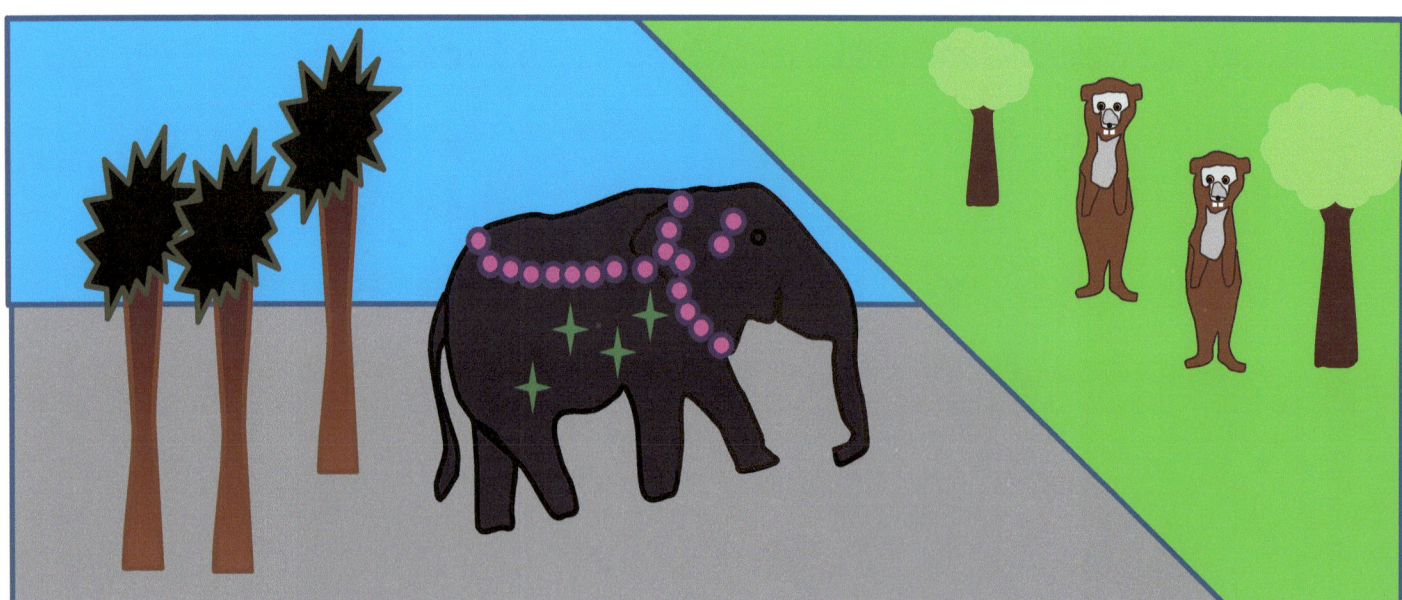

They were now walking down Madam Kruzabella Lane. The atmosphere was gloomy and the trees weren't as pretty as the trees were in Rainbow Frost. The closer they got the more they were afraid.

Rain swayed pushing them back and forth but they continued their journey. All of a sudden a bolt of lightning blazed the sky, "Boom"! They all screamed clamping onto Sooney. Sooney was such a tall elegant leader. She kept marching through the fierce weather.

From a distance, they heard a scream of a little girl coming from the river.

"Help, help!" shouted the little girl.

They all ran over toward the river. The little girl was Elica Bee.

"Help!" she shouted again from the fierce river.

"Oh no, she's just trying to trick us!" shouted Nippy and Jippy.

"No. I think she needs our help," said the twins.

Sooney found a vine attached to an old large tree. She wrapped the end of the vine around her trunk. Sooney attempted to remove the vine but the tree yanked it back. Sooney went into a tug of war match with the tree because she had a little girl to save. Every time Sooney attempted to pull the vine, the tree pulled even harder.

It was time for Sooney to use what she's expressed so hard to others and that was faith.  This time when she pulled, there was no doubt in her mind that she couldn't remove the vine.  The tree used all of his natural might but Sooney's faith exceeded the tree's natural brute strength. Sooney removed the vine.

The tree was furious shouting with a deep loud voice, "No, no, no, no!"

Sooney ran over to the twins.  Ruby and Diamond grab the end of the vine from Sooney's trunk and tossed it into the river.  Elica grabbed the vine and Sooney heist her up to safety.

Elica started to run off but then she stopped and walked back over to them.

"Thank you for saving my life" said Elica Bee.

The twins shook her hand and replied, "You're welcome."

"Elica Beeeeeeee!" shouted a lady with a voice that echoed from afar.

Elica wanted to stay with them, but she didn't want to face the madam's wrath. She ran, then jumped on her horse, and took off speedily. The girls were now concerned about Elica Bee and they knew that they had to get to Mount Frost very soon.

Mount Frost was creepy.  Kruzabella's palace was very visible and her voice was as loud as can be. It echoed throughout the mountain so loud that the mountain would crack at times.

Everyone eased their way closer and closer.  Nippy and Jippy's teeth chattered like never before.  Sooney would get behind them at times to root them on to keep pressing forward.

They were now in the presence of Mount Frost.

"Well, well, well, look who we have here!" shouted Jelica Bee standing right behind them with her wand in her right hand.

Everyone turned around to face her.

"Jelica Bee we don't want any trouble," said Diamond.

"Oh yes you do because you're on my turf now!" shouted Jelica.

Jelica Bee pointed her wand forcefully to let out the stingy bees but before she could unleash them Elica Bee ran up and snatched the wand out of her sister's hand.

"What are you doing Elica?  These are the enemies," said Jelica.

"Jelica, these aren't the enemies.  They saved my life," replied Elica.

"I see that we have a little trader!" shouted Madam Kruzabella as she walked up out of the darkness.

Everyone sighed. They expected to see a mean old lady resembling a witch but Madam Kruzabella was very beautiful. Her long gorgeous spongy hair flowed in the wind. Her lips were colored with red and her gown was long and elegant. The more she spoke, she wasn't as beautiful as she seemed. She was very mean and her heart was cold as a frozen ice cycle hanging off the side of a mountain. Outside beauty isn't always what it seems.

The real beauty is what's on the inside sweet and pleasant as a butterfly floating in the spring. As beauty passes it transfers from one to another forming smiles, but the presence of Madam Kruzabella made the atmosphere unpleasant. She snatched Elica by the arm!

"Jelica Bee, grab your wand and unleash the stingy bees!" Kruzabella shouted.

Jelica Bee was confused because she didn't want to disobey the madam but on the other hand she didn't want her sister to get hurt.

"Jelica what's taking you so long?" asked Kruzabella.

Jelica Bee rushed over to grab her wand. Her hand was trembling uncontrollably with fear. Jelica pointed her wand with her eyes closed tightly. It was clear that she didn't want to unleash the stingy bees but she was afraid.

"Give me that!" shouted Kruzabella snatching the wand away from Jelica.

Nippy and Jippy teeth chattered out of control. Jippy fainted.

Kruzabella pointed the wand and shouted, "Unleash the stingy bees!"

Sooney wanted to come to their rescue but it wasn't her fight.

"Stingy bees!" shouted Nippy.

She put Jippy on her back running off to safety. Everyone else scattered except for Ruby, Diamond, and Sooney. Sooney inched up close behind the twins.

She whispered in Ruby and Diamonds ears saying, "Faith."

The twin princesses picked up their sparkly batons and pointed them at Madam Kruzabella.

"I command you to stop!" Ruby and Diamond shouted.

Nothing happened. The stingy bees were getting closer, and the girls were puzzled.

"No, no, no, don't be afraid," said Sooney guiding the girls along.

The girls pointed their sparkly batons again saying, "I command you to stop!"

Nothing happened and the girls were discouraged.

"We can't do this," said the twins.

"Yes you can.  Close your eyes and believe," said Sooney whispering into the twins ears.

The girls closed their eyes.  They were determined.  Fear vanished and boldness entered.  They were on one accord.

"We command you to stop!" shouted Ruby and Diamond.

Butterflies floated out of their sparkly batons.  They pushed the stingy bees back into Jelica Bee's wand and formed a circle around Kruzabella locking her in.

Ruby and Diamond had a little time to unlock the Great Rainbow Light. The twins jumped onto Sooney's back.

"Sooney wait! Elica and Jelica come with us," said the twins.

Elica Bee jumped on the back of her horse. Jelica looked back and forth from Kruzabella who was still entrapped in the center of the butterflies.

"Don't you dare!" said Kruzabella gritting her teeth.

Jelica's face was flushed with fear because she knew what wrath Madam Kruzabella could bring.

"Don't listen to her," said Elica with compassion for her twin sister.

Jelica's love for her sister sealed the final decision. Jelica Bee jumped on her horse and high fived Elica Bee.

"Yee haw!" shouted Elica and Jelica.

They all headed toward the Great Rainbow Light.

Kruzabella was furious!

"Elica Bee, Jelica Bee, wait until I get my hands on you!" shouted Madam Kruzabella echoing through the mountains.

She tried and tried to get out of the circle of butterflies but she couldn't. Ruby and Diamond had minutes to make it to the Great Rainbow Light.

The butterflies faded away. Kruzabella jumped on a horse and galloped her way to stop them. She unleashed the stingy bees. Hearing the buzzing sound, the girls had to hurry.

They finally made it to the cave. Sooney stood in the doorway accompanied by the two horses while Elica and Jelica lead the twins to the Great Rainbow Light that was hidden.

"Hurry!" Sooney shouted.

Elica and Jelica opened a secret wall. There was a wall with glistening iridescent rocks. It had two locks sitting in the center of the rocks but there was a problem. The locks were too high up. Elica and Jelica ran to get Sooney.

"Sooney, Princess Ruby and Princess Diamond need you," said Elica.

"The locks are too high up!" said Jelica.

Sooney rushed over to the girls. She heists Ruby up to the first lock. Ruby unlocked it.

As Sooney lowered Ruby to the ground, they all heard the sound of buzzing bees. There was Madam Kruzabella. Sooney quickly heist Diamond up to the lock, but she stumbled onto Sooney's back.

"Hurry!" shouted Sooney.

Madam Kruzabella and the buzzing bees were getting closer and closer. Diamond looked back and forth from Madam Kruzabella to the lock. Diamond stood up with trembling hands. She took her hand and attempted to put the key into the lock but was unsuccessful.

"You can do it Diamond," said Sooney.

"Remember to have faith," said Ruby.

"Yeah," said Elica and Jelica.

Madam Kruzabella was now in arms reach.  Diamond stuck the key into the lock and turned it.  Boom, Boom, Boom!  Fierce wind blazed throughout the mountain. The mountain trembled. Florescent lights flickered through the cracks. Kruzabella galloped through the wind out of the cave.  Sooney lead the girls to safety.  All of a sudden an imprinted face appeared in the rocks of the mountain.  It was Mr. Mountain Frost.  He let out the rainbow gate forming it gradually.  Then he spotted Madam Kruzabella.  He huffed; he puffed, and blew her out of Rainbow frost!

Madam Kruzabella tried and tried to get back in, but she couldn't. The gate was locked and she could no longer enter.

Mr. Mountain Frost blew with all of his might on the piece of Rainbow Frost that was taken away by Madam Kruzabella.

Madam Kruzabella Lane was once again Frost Berry Lane. The once forbidden piece of land was now vibrant and beautiful. Ruby and Diamond had conquered Madam Kruzabella.

"Hip Hurray!" shouted the people of Rainbow Frost as they ran out of their hiding spaces.

An echoing loud voice came from the midst of the mountain saying, "Princess Ruby and Princess Diamond. I would like to present to you golden medals for your hard work!"

It was Mr. Mountain Frost himself loud and proud to be in the presence of such brave little girls.

"Well done," said a familiar voice walking up behind them.

When the twins turned around, their mother and father were standing behind them. The girls ran up to the king and queen giving them a hug.

"Well hello King Jerome and Queen Gloria," said Mr. Mountain Frost.

"Hello," replied the king and queen.

"You must be proud of such wonderful daughters," said Mr. Mountain Frost.

"We are," replied the king and queen.

Sooney loaded the girls onto her back. All of Ruby and Diamond's friends were sad but they knew that they had to return to Agape Island.

"Ruby, Diamond, can we go with you?" asked Elica and Jelica Bee.

Ruby and Diamond looked at their mother and father.

"My sister longed for a child but she never could conceive. I think you girls will be a great blessing in her and her husband's life. So that means yes," said Queen Gloria.

Elica Bee and Jelica Bee were so happy that they were finally going to have a family. They jumped on the back of their horses wildly.

"Yee haw!" Elica and Jelica shouted.

They all headed to the sparkly chest to take them back to Agape Island.

www.ingramcontent.com/pod-product-compliance
Lightning Source LLC
Chambersburg PA
CBHW041556120626
46551CB00002B/227

*9780692575802*